T0116796

THE TELEPORT CONSPIRACY

By

Elikem Adonoo

Order this book online at www.trafford.com
or email orders@trafford.com

Most Trafford titles are also available at major online book retailers.

Printed in the United States of America.

ISBN: 978-1-4269-9522-4 (sc)
ISBN: 978-1-4269-9525-5 (e)

Trafford rev. 09/08/2011

 www.trafford.com

North America & international
toll-free: 1 888 232 4444 (USA & Canada)
phone: 250 383 6864 ♦ fax: 812 355 4082

It's not all as it seems, for centuries man has believed the power of science and technology came about as a result of the betterment of goodwill of mankind in the hope of liberating us from the adverse effects of dysfunctional beliefs and culture. How did science ever come about? Was it the will of the unknown beings or mankind himself? One thing I do know for sure underlying all the facade of science, lays the dormant entity of magic which is as old as the earth, and would prevail long after the time of man passes.

-Elikem Adonoo

Chapter 1

The sun stroked the surface window of a tube train, but its heat could not be felt. So the man sitting next to the window tucked his head into his jacket to get some warmth. Standing next to him, another man was holding a newspaper dated February 22, 2065. The train was actually full of people commuting to work in the morning. The train stopped at the sound of a horn.

"Oi, Axel wakeup we're at our stop" but there was no response. Axel McAllister was fast asleep in his own perfect world where anything was possible. Seeing there was no response Chuck nudged his friend in the ribs and Axel yawned aloud with pain.

"Ouch, dude, you know that hurt. How long was I asleep for?" Axel complained.

"Well, let's see that would be the whole trip. Yeah, you slept through it all. Hey but we're not late for our appointment." Chuck blurted out.

Axel and Chuck are both juniors at the University of Warwick, Coventry with a plan to change the course of physics. Their destination was Oxford faculty of science. Earlier on they were refused a grant to undertake their research. The future looked a bit grim for the young students. The doors of the train opened and they stepped out into the cold. The winter cold was more than enough to dampen their spirits. Axel walked with caution as he approached the stairs because earlier at college he tripped and fell, spraining his ankle, although, he felt a bit better now. This all happened when this freshman caught his eyes. He had been wanting to ask her out but didn't know how to just yet. He thought she was special and needed a different wooing approach. All the girls on campus he had been out with; all wanted one thing and that was one night stands and he was looking for a steady relationship.

As they went up the stairs, Chuck brought out the map-digitized plate to locate a position the source contact they were supposed to meet. He was an informant working at the University of Oxford as a spy for the two young Warwick hopeful students. They came out of the train station onto the main street which was full of pubs, shops, banks and some other obscure offices. It was a day like no other in Oxford, freezing and nobody in sight to ask for directions.

"Are you sure we're at the right allay, Chuck? You reckon there is a pub called Piccadilly here?" Axel asked confused looking the direction sign.

"He said it would be around Debenhams shop, but the location is not on the map. Do you reckon we have been bamboozled? I just don't believe this, first the grant board back at school, now this. There is no point in this venture Axel. He winced in disgust at the sight of failure as he sat on the strip of the sidewalk.

"Don't say that Chuck. You know as well as I do that success comes as a result of great perseverance. We've done our part of the bargain; it's now the turn of society to do their part. The reason they had for refusing our claim of the direction of physics is not their fault, its evolution. Our experiment could be a threat to the world at large. We do not know the implications until we've received the x-factor. If the informant loved our idea and stood us up by not coming to the rendezvous, it's not the end of the world. We can try another source and perhaps take more time to revise the formula."

By this time Chuck diverted his concentration to a cue ball that generated heat when it was touched. That way you don't have to pocket your hands all the time. "God knows I don't want to give up but you know it's frustrating"

"We have to get out of this cold, dude or our balls would not make it. It's like -20 outside here. Spending 3 hours in a train it's annoyingly gruesome to just go back home." Axel squirmed.

"Don't worry about that. I do remember Aunt Rose lives around the next lane. We could get some hot coffee."

The two continued on the trek to find Aunt Rose's house. Cars were parked by the roadside with one school girl busily kissing her boyfriend; their lips were practically glued to each other. Chuck did not see this but Axel called his attention to it. Upon seeing the school girl, his jaw dropped and stared with astonishment. "Hey, what's wrong, do you know her from anywhere?"

"What do mean about that! That's Millicent, my cousin"

"Oops, sorry didn't know"

"That's the house right here, I've not seen her in a long while that's all. She is looking really mature. But what is she doing with that older jog-looking bloke. I mean she is only about 14 I reckon. Maybe I should go there and interrupt them... well you know she is just too young to be making out with that guy. I reckon he would be about 18 at least.

Chuck made gestures to walk towards the car but Axel stopped him. "Let's get inside dude it's freezing out here. You could tell her mum though...hope she is home."

As they walked onto the front of the house, the door opened and out walked Aunt Rose looking surprised to see his nephew. "Oh, my goodliness Chucky James, is that really you?"

"Hello there, Aunt Rose, you are indeed looking as smashing as ever. Me and my friend here were in this part of town and decided to pay you a visit"

Well, don't just stand there, come on inside, I'll fix you a hot cup of coffee, yeah.

Chuck and Axel looked at each other and giggled together quietly. They both stepped inside which was incredibly warm and comfortable. Aunt Rose was rather chubby looking as compared to her daughter, who was quite thin.

"What brings you to this part of town, Chucky?" Aunt Rose asked as she poured the coffee into their cups.

Upon thinking about the secrecy of their research, revealing their plans to his aunt would only make things worse. This is because both of the juniors thought the world was not ready to see the intricate details of the experiment. After all, their plan would lead to the revolution of the world as we know it. At this time in the year 2065, there have been a countless number of advancements in all spectrums of science. So fleeting has been this development it has led to improvements in eradication of viral diseases like the common flu, HIV/AIDS, bird and swine flu, and even now in the 21st century AD a new kind of germ has emerged that is tougher and more resistant to kill than a virus. But that is not the worry these days, everyday; scientists are claiming new remedies such as vaccines and cures to strengthen the human immune system and those of other animals.

The major problem in this era is not diseases but a much worse crisis. Terrorism has risen to catastrophic levels. Here, right now over the past 10 years. 250,000 aeroplanes and 4 million cars have been bombed statistically speaking. Everyone around the world is living in fear as they all have an equal chance of being targeted. Nobody is safe at the moment. Solutions must be found fast or else the human race will struggle to annihilate each other. The threat to society was long believed that the human race would die when the last tree dies. This is now a cliché.

Outside of the home of Aunt Rose, it started to snow. The comrades looked at each other with a grim expression on their faces. They both hoped of meeting the contact who did not show up which messed up their day. On top of that it started to snow, how would they get back to college now? They had a lot of assignments that needed submission the following day and not to mention the project they were working on.

The front door opened once more and in walked the lovely Millicent, looking as satisfied as ever from making out with her boyfriend. She was still in her uniform and the top buttons on her blouse looked like it was unbuttoned in a rush. Her mum caught sight of her and stared at her cautiously.

"Millie, why are you now coming home, hah, its half past 8pm. You are supposed to be doing your homework by now. Oh, so you have been out there kissing that bloody bum all day, haven't you? You know sometimes I feel I can't take anymore of your sordid behaviour. I feel you are rushing through life too quickly, dear. When I was your age I never could entertain the thought of kissing my boyfriend, yet alone an older boyfriend who can't go out with girls his own age." Aunt Rose shook her head as she said that.

"Oh, come off it mum, your time was different from mine. Besides Billy and I were just talking; that's all." Millie blurted out to her weary mother.

"Mmph, hahaaha, man this girl is good." Axel giggled to himself. He was listening to their conversation with the door closed in the kitchen. Chuck was busily sipping his coffee and not paying attention to his buddy's idiosyncrasies.

Upon entering the kitchen to fix herself a quick snack. Millie came across Axel who was presumably trying to fake picking up something by the door.

"Hey, who are you?"

"Sorry, we had to meet like this little lady I was just trying to pick up my keys. You know they fell right by the door side. I have heard a lot about you though."

"You haven't answered my question. Who are you really? Because if you are a burglar, it would take me only 2 seconds to call the police." Millie was now advancing backwards inching nearer to the telephone.

At that same moment both Chuck and Aunt Rose walked into the kitchen. "I see you have met my college mate, Cousin Millie?"

"Wow, it's you. So you do know this moron?"

"Watch your language young lady; I'm this close to putting my hands on you, show some respect, will you. That's Chucky's friend you're talking to."

"No mum, that's a freaking nobody who just doesn't know how to express himself. Look I'm off to bed. I don't need all this drama." Her mother looked disgusted as she said that, and off she went upstairs. "I'm so sorry for that Axel, usually she'd not behave like that."

"No offense, mum. Might have been my fault actually." Axel murmured to himself.

"What's that you said, I didn't catch that? Well never mind her, you know it's snowing and I reckon it would probably be difficult for the two of you to get back to school, at this moment. I'd suggest you spend the night here. Don't worry; I'd just prepare the guest room for you now." She left the two of them alone for the mean time to tend to the guest room upstairs right next to Millie's. As she passed by her daughter's room, she was fast asleep. Thoughts skimmed through her mind about the plight of her child that just made her so worried. After a while she moved on.

The two comrades both contemplated on their day. Sincerely, they both thought it did not go well. But the question in their mind was why did the informant not show up? What happened to him? Or did he decide just to play a prank on them that he could lend a hand in the fight for their noble cause. All these thoughts disturbed the two hopefuls. How on earth were they going to get the x-factor? A chemical compound so rare and more valuable than uranium and plutonium combined, that the mere production of it cost the GDP of a developing country. It was a strange chemical though, non-toxic to the human body and invisible under a ray of light. Its main use to its developers was not fully known, but to Axel its use was insurmountable leading to the eradication of one problem and that was teleportation.

CHAPTER 2

A man suddenly started walking briskly towards the road with a look of pain on his face. The road had just been cleared of snow and looked pretty icy. The unknown man fell sideways but got up immediately after that. The reason for his fastidiousness is soon to be known as two other men from way behind starting yelling curses after the hurt man. Apparently he had been short at close range near the abdomen, he held the injured part with his hand stopping the blood from gushing out. His best interest was to hide. The two assassins were on his tale and it all looked very grim for him. The street was actually pit black with an air of death. They actually closed in on him. A look of satisfaction descended on the face of the thugs. Both of them reached into their jackets to bring about the doom of this man in pain. But something strange happened in a split splash second, a bus pulled by right beside the alley the injured man was hiding. And then, with the last ounce of energy in his body, the man dived headfirst into the bus. Just right then the two thugs fired shots at the former place the man had lied down at. They run after the bus throwing a huge amount of curses at it.

"You are finished McCain, we know where you live and you have no place to hide. Wherever you go we're going to find you and put a dozen bullets in you…, you piece of shit. Damn you, McCain." the thug screamed these words out as he redrew the gun back into his jacket. His partner looked at him with a smug grin and spoke three cold words.

"Retrieve to headquarters"

"What! No agent 17, we got the sad bum bloke. Our best interest is to follow him and put him out of his misery for good. Your last shot hit him square and he would survive it if we don't finish what we started"

"How dare you, agent 18. Definitely you do know that I outrank you in every sense of our line of duty."

18 stopped talking immediately, and looked as though he had been slapped in the face. These two men were a ruthless bunch of an organized crime syndicate. They were dressed in black and wearing dark sunglasses. The one called 17 was even more ruthless and sly-looking.

"You have caused too much of a nuisance 18, look all around you there people watching our every move as we even speak. And you keep on babbling about that old fool trying to steal the x-factor. We've recovered this rear item back into the hands of the Shadow Law Organization, and it would be in our best interests to return the x-factor." he said with a slight bit of satisfaction on his face.

"Well, I guess you are right, 17. Wow, I reckon the other agents would be gloating with envy when the boss gets to know that we've recovered the x-factor back into the hands of the organization. Man, think about it, we might even be promoted into the feared regiment of the Shadow Law.

As these two intrepid men stepped into their car as it automatically found them as if it knew where they were. Moments later they took off at full speed with an air of despair as the earth was in for a ride that it had not experienced before.

Human evolution as it has always maintained itself has gone by one adage and that is that: history always keeps repeating itself. But not this time, there is a new element called the x-factor. Of course but this element has always existed before even the beginning of time and yet the Shadow Law Organization has always known of its use and purpose, yet they are a group that has sworn an oath of secrecy and have the power to eliminate anyone who got in their way. They had superior technology and always chose their members from the elite breeds of unique human beings with an uncanny skill for chaos. Their interest is to see to it the human race is flooded with an air of ignorance and never fully understanding the solutions to the problems until it was late and it was no longer needed anymore.

Over the past 3000 years, there has been a breach in the functioning of the Shadow Law Organization, their members saw to it that no more will humans stay in the main frame as weakling to the point of not fully knowing the solutions to their problems. These new members of the Shadow Law Organization formed a small elite team of the good-willed and forcefully broke away in a massive revolution in the otherworld. So fierce was this war that it led to the death of its mentor, but that did not stop them. Before he died the then mentor called Master Khan laid down the 3 Rules of Vivo and named his successor as his eldest son, Magi who also played his path as his father had willed. So it was set the balance had been tilted and the otherworld was split into two unequal halves with the Shadow law Organization having two thirds control of the earth and the White Lighter Organization by Master Khan having control of the remaining.

So the steads of time were set and the course of history under the influence of the Shadow Law Organization. Throughout the course of time, these two sides of the otherworld have waved wars on each other, each with the desire to rule the earth for good with no interference from each other. So far Shadow Law (shadows as they preferably called in their world) was in control but could merely keep this balance as the White lighters were always waging war to defend the interests of mankind. The Shadow Law elemental is actually purely evil and they feed on the ignorance of mankind. They need humans to survive and the more ignorant humans are the more powerful they get.

However, forever ingrained in the hearts of the white lighters were the Three Rules of Vivo, Master Khan put it in place before he died and his son was of the few left to champion his ideas into making humans survive and thrive in their environment. Well all we know now is that yes, Magi had indeed led the right cause of his father. But there is a glitch to all this, these rules could only be used twice every millennia within a period of 500 years in between each other before it could actually work. The great leader Master Khan saw it fit to ingrain the rules at the back of the palm of every white lighter that joined their noble cause. These rules were incomprehensible to the average human but in the hands of the white lighter they could enter the minds of the unconscious human mind and make them see the truth about the intricate design of the universe and use it to their advantage in the betterment of mankind in all spectrums of technology and science.

Over the course of history, brilliant minds such as Galileo, Newton and Einstein emerged and changed the course of human nature with their ideas. A number of countless others followed suit which led to evolution of society at large. In no time the world of science arrived coupled with the birth of technology as its vessel. From this point society got better with improvements in healthcare, medicine, travel, logistics, education and politics.

But how did this happen? Where did the great thinkers of the past worlds able to get their ideas from? It all started from the Ancients Greeks such as Hippocrates and Aristotle down to Romans, the Anglo-Saxons and then the Germans. And with the lust of power of the Germans, they abused it and almost destroyed the world as we know it during the World War II. But the white lighters maintained the balance and helped the great mind Einstein overcome the world war by letting him see insight of the truth of the art of war. Hence Einstein joined allies with the Americans and supplied them with knowledge the Magi had given him through his dreams. Only in a dream can the white lighters impact their knowledge and the subjects are not aware of the events in their dream.

As was said, it was Magi who chose Einstein to carry out the faith of mankind and save the course of history from the cruel Nazis of the WWII.

The Three Rules of Vivo were thus as ingrained in holy words as:

1. White Lighters must only impact knowledge through dreams.

2. White Lighters must reveal the unconscious mind if necessary.

3. Only Magi can subvert the former 2 Rules of Vivo by deciding the faith of mankind.

So those were the Three Rules of Vivo put in place by Master Khan, father of Magi. Thus the balance exists for the best interests of man. All of man's thought is filtered by the White Lighters and accorded by the Magi. Magi, himself visited Newton, Einstein and Galileo, and laid the inspirational and complex ideas in their conscious minds. For this to work, the White Lighters must choose someone who is pure at heart and have the ability to unlock the unconscious reality into the conscious. Few are chosen randomly across the world to fulfil this task and the ones with the potent ability to believe in the awesome power of the unconscious are taken by Magi himself.

As time passed throughout the course of history the number of white lighters dwindled until at the present time they are left with only seven with Magi being their leader and god over the remaining six. As the Shadow Law continued its rampage on the extermination of the white lighters, elementals on both sides were lost with the White Light losing more members than the Shadow Law.

The difference between the two sides was that unlike the White Lighters, the Shadow Law members were able to take on human form and make human beings ignorant of the innate knowledge that they possess. They arrived on the earth since time began and earlier on inhabited lower animals and later humans. They breed on the spirit of not knowing and thrived in the conscious of all living organisms. In the beginning, lower animals do not have minds and so did they also. As millions of millennia passed these shadows of the Shadow Law as they were called also evolved as humans emerged out of the earlier primates such as the homo family of species. With their new found power to be able to dwell in the conscious minds of humans they developed into catastrophic demonic entities living side by side laying the path of the wayward sons of men into the realm called the otherworld. Master Khan was one of their illustrious followers until one day upon enlightenment he seized to go by Shadow's ways. To achieve this aim Khan had to cast the evil side of the shadow out of his being to become a White Light and saviour of earth. More followers also received enlightenment and joined the noble and true cause of Master Khan and through that his son was born.

The Shadow Law on earth appeared in the physical and formed an organization on earth which possessed the x-factor which they knew would lead to their demise. Back on earth the stakes were set and the young man Axel McAllister and his friend were being watched with keen interest by the Shadow Law and the White Light. It was in the best interest of the shadows to eliminate the two young men, but Magi would not let that happen if he could help it.

CHAPTER 3

The university campus of Warwick looked gloomy as the clouds descended with rain. The lecture halls were all packed full with students some seemed vulnerable to the ways their lectures handled complex subjects as they could not fully grasp the concepts and others had a flair with the way the professor handled the course of the subject as they understood it perfectly. Among those that grasped the subject fully was Axel McAllister and those that did not was Chucky James. Chucky actually struggled with the subject of quantum physics and always looked forward to the guidance of Axel, his best friend. The two actually practically needed each other as in the sense that Chucky had a way of wooing the ladies at college and Axel had a way with books. At a young age, Axel had developed an esoteric mind of grasping complex subjects such as quantum physics quite easily. He could read huge books at an alarming short time and recite it back to back without leaving out the intricate details. The subject of physics fascinated the young lad since the age of 8 since the day his father disappeared without a trace. He always had the uncanny idea of somehow bringing him back from wherever he was.

**

Time was set back into the past and there stood a young boy of 8 with his father. Peter McAllister looked in every way as his son and both had a look of compassion edged on their foreheads. They appeared to be packing some stuff that looked like fishing equipment. Unlike his father, young Axel had freckles on his chick. And there was a woman holding a lunch bag that contained turkey sandwiches who was supposedly Axels' mum.

"Oh how I wish I could join you boys" Jane McAllister admitted as she put the package containing the sandwiches into the boot of the car with the rest of the fishing equipment. The boot was closed as the car was sparked to life, Peter gave his dear wife a kiss and then sped off young Axel saying: "Bye, mummy."

"Bye, Ax" his mum chuckled with zeal as she said goodbye to her son.

The drive to the lake took about 20 minutes for them to get to the river. The weather was actually sultry but there was not a single fisherman in sight, that was actually odd. But the one and the half man had no clue as to what was going to happen to them. The car stopped by the packing spot near the river. They took out their equipment and lunch and embarked on the fleet journey to the bank of the river. As they started to hoist their baits on the hooks, a bizarre thing happened to the weather all of a sudden, it was no longer sultry and quiet. But was a loud boom and there formed a thick grey cloud with thunder and lightning. A huge massive wage of energy hit the bank right at the spot Axel stood with his father. And there stood two men who had an air of death in their looks. These two men were Agents 17 and 18.

"We have come for you, Mr McAllister." 17 said this as he drew out his arm in accordance.

"But who are you and what did you want with me? And my son needs his father, definitely you can't take me away. I've done nothing" as Peter said this, he threw his arms around his son as to protect him from these strange men from nowhere. As he continued asking questions with fear the two agents started laughing.

"Ei, 17 you think he's scared, he's not aware that it's his son that we actually want." 18 let out a demonic smile as he stopped laughing.

"Look here you schmuck, it's the boy we want, not you. Now hand him over or we'll vaporize you to dust. You have 40 seconds.

Axel stood there behind his father as if he had been frozen. At that instant minute, Peter McAllister acted quickly and told this last few words to his son.

"Now listen to me, Ax, I'll take on these two men. The moment I do, you take off at full speed. No matter what happens I'll always be behind son." Axel still hadn't recovered from the shock and still looked as though he was numb.

"Go on, boy move it now" His father screamed as he launched a full attack on these on the agent called 18. The punch hit 18 square in the face and he was yelling with pain. After that Peter tried taking on agent 17 but alas he was too fast. Peter McAllister hit the bank floor hard but would not allow himself to be defeated, at least not now when his son was still standing there awestruck with fear.

"Axel, run, run, ... run now." Peter yelled out to his son.

"But daddy…" Recovering from the shock the young Axel started to pace backwards.

Agent 18 had now recovered from his punch and at that moment took out his laser gun. "You'll regret ever punching me in the face, you cretin." Just at that instant 17 stopped the blast from the laser gun and absorbed it into his bare palm. With the expressionless look on his face, it seems he did not feel a thing.

"Go after the boy, he's gaining ground and he's the primary target. Don't you forget that 18. As for the father I'll deal with him personally." 18 acted at once with no excuse and went after the young Axel who was now lost in the woods near the river.

"Please, he's just a child leave him out of it." Peter groaned in pain as the agent poured on him what seems to be a fluid of blue colour and immediately Peter started to disintegrate. Within moments, he burned up into smoke as if he wasn't there in the first place.

***

Mr McAllister, Mr McAllister,… oi, are you bloody with us? Axel came back to really as if he had just been into a trance. "Surely, my dear lad it's too early to be day-dreaming now, isn't it?

"I'm sorry, professor I just slipped into a mind maze of my own creation" he sat up straight as he replied his lecturer.

"Well, well fine my dear lad. Would you be so kind as to explain the Einstein theory of the relativity of the motion of an atom? I'm afraid it just escaped me a little bit there." The old cocky professor stroked his head as these two words escaped his lips. Just then the whole class started to giggle at the professor's dismay. Axel then got up and took the class by storm to no surprise of the rest of the class as he always delivered.

CHAPTER 4

The bell chimed as the clock struck the 11th hour as the students looked weary as exam time was upon them. The main library was packed with students from wall to wall. All the corridors were also packed with students in study groups planning their course of action in their exams. Others used their time sparingly and visited the sick bay to get more time off for the paper they were to write the following week. But far in the dorms was Axel and Chuck in their rooms. Chuck was practically memorizing formulae notes from most of his previous lectures and murmuring under his breath, whereas Axel on the other hand decided to focus on other issues in his head as to whether there was any other substitute to the x-factor. He had worked out the right formula for his invention but it had to be tested. And then there was another issue of the informant having the x-factor not showing up. Several days had actually passed since the day the informant supposedly stood them up.

As the two young lads pondered about their affairs, the phone rang and both jumped up in alarm. The phone hadn't ringed in a long time since things got a little bit hot on campus. And then both realized that it was Axels' mobile phone that was ringing. He then reached out and grabbed his phone, and then at that instant the phone transformed into a person's face that spoke.

"I don't believe this, is that you Mr. Jacobson? We thought you stood us up. Why didn't you meet us at the rendezvous like you said… What you were followed and shot." At this point Chuck got interested and lowered his book down. After waiting for the conversation to end, he jumped off the bed and started firing questions at his mate.

"Don't tell me that was him." Axel stared at his friend and nodded in agreement.

"Well don't just stand there tell me why he stood us up." Axel was somehow in shock just as the day his father disappeared out of the bloom. His friend came closer to him and waved his hand across his face. "What is the matter with you? Come on come out of it."

"Sit down Chuck, there is something I've to tell you." Axel looked quite serious as these words left his mouth and he began to tell the mysterious story of how one unusual day his father had disappeared, the police asked him all sorts of questions which he answered as the way things happened. But the police couldn't figure out a clue as to what the boy talked about. In his report archive, the detective recommended that he should be taken in for psychiatric evaluation. They probably thought he was in shock as to the way his father disappeared without a trace. The police report of the incident found no traces of blood or any sign of struggle that showed that Mr. Peter McAllister had been abducted or killed. But where was his body, there was no trace of it anywhere. His car was parked right outside off-road of the fishing bank. Axel reported that two unidentified men came out of nowhere and commanded his father that they were after him. His father tried protecting him but he was outmatched in every possible way. One of the unknown men then started chasing Axel but lost him in the nick of the woods. His mother was heartbroken and never gave up looking for her husband. And yet as time went on his memory faded in their hearts, although Mrs McAllister never married and Axel withdrew into his own world of creating something that could bring his father back from the void. He was the only one who saw what happened, he knew the police didn't buy his story, but that did not matter to him. Since the time as a young boy, Axel always recollected his dreams of building the teleport device. Dream after dream, he put the notes down over the course of the years until he got into the university. Because of the nature and structure of his mind, he was able to put the missing pieces of the puzzle bit by bit over the years together to form one solid design of the teleport device.

Axel knew that telling this story to his friend would seem awkward but he still went on anyway. After all had been said Chuck still looked confused with what that got to do with Jacobson not showing.

"Don't you see that Chuck, these two men are the men who abducted my father years ago. No doubt about it, and he said that they took the x-factor from him. That was the sole purpose they were after him"

"Oh, I get it. It means we're dead. We have two strange dudes with a bad attitude after us. Sorry about that mate and you still don't know the real reason they are after us. I knew this dream of yours of building this device would get us into trouble." Chuck complained to his friend.

"Come now that's not the point of it. Don't let these two scare you. They have something I want and I'm going to get it back. It seems they think they have got me in their trap. Now is the time to find answers to my past and find the mystery about the two men who abducted my father and why they have taken the x-factor."

"Well, how are you going to do that? It's not like they live round the corner, you know." Chuck tried reasoning with his friend to back out of the project but Axel turned and answered him with these three mysterious words: "In my dreams."

CHAPTER 5

On the other side of the earthly realm called the otherworld. The Shadow Law watched with keen interest as the young lad they had tried kidnapping was getting to know what was going on. There was a mist of death surrounding the elementals of the Shadow Law. In their realm they had no bodies but floated around in what seemed to be a grey smoke with a pair of eyes that spoke cold words of despair. They were created as such that they fed on the ignorance of men. Whenever there was an age when man was becoming ignorant the Shadow Law elementals grew very strong and were able to break loose from their otherworld realm which for them was like a prison. They envied what mankind had and always wished to subjugate the earth with their cruel ways and end the time of mankind. But now there were a lot of problems on their heads; not of just the boy but now Magi and the other white lighters were gaining strength in their numbers and were an impending treat to them the original elementals. To deal with this new threat, the heads of the Shadow Law elementals called forth a meeting and all their members were summoned, even those on earth in their human form were attending the meeting. The two agents called 17 and 18 had left their earthly bodies, and were highly expected to be at the meeting since they had reclaimed the x-factor. But this x-factor could not be brought into the otherworld of the elementals, henceforth it was in a secured location only known to the two agents. The purpose of their meeting was to detect how to bring a stop to Magi and his followers and destroy the boy once and for all. The shadow law elementals were now disenchanted with the way the things were going and met to look for a solution. The otherworld realm in human sense actually did not exist, but if a human were to picture it in his head it looked something like a deserted mountain with holes scattered evenly all the sides but none at the apex. As soon as the meeting started this mountain began to shake like a volcano and immense grey smoke erupted from all the sides and flowed into the air. There were thousands of them surrounding the whole mountain which now looked pitch dark. The smoke developed eyes and now started to chant the holy name of their leaders who appeared at the apex. And these were the leaders behind the shadow law organization, four in number. Their smoke was much bigger than those at the bottom of the summit of the mountain and their eyes were glowing as if it was on fire. After attaining their full form, the first leader began to speak.

"Most of you know why we are gathered here this period. We have an impending menace on our smoke and we need to put our flames together in order to solve it. All our efforts to curb the army that Magi is nurturing..."

At the moment, when Magi's name was mentioned, all the other members of the shadows shivered and wailed in pain. They feared Magi and did not speak of his name even in their own realm. It was only their leaders who were brave enough to call his name. At this moment the elder shadow elemental paused and re-examined his words before he continued his speech.

"Just look at yourselves and see what you have become. I can tell that if the humans were to know of our existence they would have pitied us and mocked us in shame. Our very enemies now have allies in their mist in the form of Magi, and the moment I mention his name you all shiver as if he's some kind of higher power far greater than us. Do you not know yourselves fellow shadows, we are far stronger and more equipped than these flimsy white lighters and their ways. As a matter of fact, you all know that they can't even take on human forms like we do. Their only influence on humans is through their dreams."

At this point of the meeting, among the four shadow leaders, the second leader took over the speech of the first leader, its voice rather a bit different from the first leader as it was ice-cold and bitter.

"And that's the purpose of this meeting, fellow shadows. We are here today to put an end to the abysmal behaviour of our traitors who call themselves the white lighters. We have finally procured the very item the white lighters believe would bring an end to our very existence, and for that we would not stand by and let this happen. Nieska and Salmon, I believe both of you have good news for us all at this meeting. What say you, I grant you power to speak, servant?

All the other shadow elementals turned their eyes to the position of the smoke that floated close to the base of the mountain. There were two of them, agent 17 was the one called Nieska and 18 the one referred to as Salmon who was the clumsy.

In its elemental form, agent 17 was not as bold and intrepid as he was on earth when he vanquished the father of young Axel McAllister, although that day he was not able to get what he wanted, until several years later he and his partner intercepted the informant at the university who had the x-factor in his position and was about to hand it over to Axel. In a mere mortal's hands the x-factor was harmless but in the hands of Axel it was very deadly to the lives of the shadow law elementals. As Nieska and Salmon were given the opportunity to speak at the gathering, both of their smoke merged together to form one solid mass of a purple gas that glowed with four green eyes. Without this fusion, they could not communicate to the higher shadow law elementals that were very powerful and needed a strong energy to talk to. As they finished fusing they became stronger in form and bolder to talk to their leaders.

"Yes, your lordships we have indeed taken claim of the x-factor and it lies hidden in a far place way beyond the reach of the human who evaded us once before as a child. His father is still in the grim-hold and he believes he could bring him back with its awesome power. So far we have not been able to locate him yet as he keeps being watched and protected by the white lighters."

The third shadow leader could not stand anymore of this nonsense and spoke with anger in its voice, "What do you mean Niesmon (i.e. the fusion name of Nieska and Salmon)? Where do you get the idea that the boy wants to use the x-factor to bring his father back? That's total rubbish, Magi controls the boys actions and thoughts, and is using him to formulate a machine that could allow instant travel across any area of earth in just an instant. It could even bring him here to our realm and put an end to us all. We are not safe, fellow shadows. The time to act is now. We must find the boy and end him before Magi shows him how he can end us."

It was now the turn of the final shadow leader to speak, and it was the most reserved and serenest but bent on immense evil upon the human race. The whole mood in the otherworld stood with an air of a solemnness and sobriety as the words of their final leader was engraved in their eyes.

"You have all heard and participated, fellow shadows. It's now clear what we must do. We must find the boy and end him before Magi uses him to end us. Leave now the otherworld and enter your human hosts on earth. Spread ignorance among them so we can feed on them to regain our strength in this world."

There was a loud noise in the otherworld after the last leader spoke. All over the mountain, the holes from which the shadow law organization elementals came out of began to glow. It seemed as if the hole was like a vacuum cleaner as it sucked the smoke which was the elementals' body in the otherworld. In a few seconds, the mountain stood as it once was before uninhabited and very quiet as it should be.

CHAPTER 6

Back on earth, near a university campus where intellectual minds engaged in conversations about the courses that were giving them problems and how they would be able to finish their project before the term ends. Others did not care a rat's ass what they were in for at school but participating in hall week celebrations; the booze and the college chicks as they so fondly called their opposite sex colleagues. But also not far from the university campus was the apartment of the young Axel McAllister and his friend, Chuck who were talking about something that had to do with dreams. The room was stacked full with quantum physics books that left a small place for the two young blokes to sit. There were far powers working somewhere that they did not know as yet but Axel had a theory that he could get in touch with them through his dreams and find solutions to his past and present problems. Chuck was in serious doubt whether as to this new plan of his friend would work for them. As they continued to talk, a book fell of the table and landed on the floor as if it had been pushed. But neither Axel nor Chuck was even close to it to push as it fell to the ground. Chuck jumped out of his chair with fright as this happened,

"What was that, did you do that?" Chuck blurted out to his friend.

"Come off it you know my hand was near that book. I told you something strange was going on, now do you believe me?" As he said these words to his friend he bent down still sitting on his chair to pick up the book. He immediately realized that the book was one of his physics 101 tutorials back when he was a freshman. Amazingly enough the book glowed as he turned the front cover and these words were engraved in it:

***

Go to sleep, Axel and close your mind to all thoughts so that I may talk to you. Oh... and tell your friend to keep watch over you as you may need him to wake you up. See you on the other side, chosen one.

***

Chuck stared at the book at all angles but he could not see these engravings that Axel read out aloud. He was totally awestruck by all these happenings.

"How come you can read it and I can't."

"I don't know but it seems they want to speak to me. You have to sit beside my bed and wake me up when the time is right. Oh shit, it didn't tell the time you should wake me up." He shook the book and asked it: "Oi... mmm book what time should my friend wake after I'm unconscious."

The book glowed once more and wrote these words:

***

Give the book to your friend, Chuck. He will know when to wake you up when the time is right. Hurry up and don't delay, it's very important. I'm waiting for you and remember to clear your mind of all your thoughts.

***

Axel didn't have to be told twice, he quickly gave the book to his friend and told him what to do. They both walked into the bedroom, Chuck took a stool and sat by the bed as his friend lied on it.

Just at the right moment, Axel went into a deep sleep and not even a normal blow to the jaw could wake him up. The only person that could do otherwise was his friend, Chuck holding the book in his hands. Now he too could also see what was in the book and amazed he was.

As Axel went deep into his unconscious, where no man could actually see there was a bright light as if he was in a tunnel. He realized that he wasn't in the room with Chuck anymore and there was a voice talking to him.

"Follow the light then you shall find me, keep to it and you wont miss me and do not listen to any other voice apart from mine."

Axel felt afraid as he heard the voice that was unknown to him, but eventually he mastered up courage and walked on into the void. As he journeyed on into the bright light, things started to happen that he could not fully understand. One moment he thought he heard his father's voice telling him to stop and take a drink of water close by the edges of the tunnel, as soon as this voice stopped speaking; he felt a strong edge to take a sip of water by the side of the tunnel. Just as he did this, a fountain spring popped out of nowhere, and out gushed water. He knelt down to take a drink to quench this insurmountable thirst that he had never felt before. Immediately as he did this, the fountain changed into a massive arm with hands that made an attempt to grab the unsuspecting Axel McAllister into the void. The hand grasped Axel's neck and pulled him in with great force and he started to yell out very hard but nobody was there to help him. Indeed he now realized that he was in great trouble, he kept on screaming because the pain in his neck was getting worse. He then reached out to grab anything to help him stop this strange hand. Just as he did so he felt the handle of a sword. He didn't have to think twice before picking it up. In just an instant he swung the blade and slashed the hand which yelled out in pain also. Consequently the grip loosened and he was free once more. He then backed away from the edge of the tunnel and stood on his feet once and the sword had now vanished into thin air. How was this possible? He thought to himself that he wouldn't stand there to find out, he took off walking but this time at full speed.

Moments later, he realized that he was getting close to the end of the tunnel. The light was very bright and it glowed as it shone on a certain man with silver coloured hair and beard. He seemed to be holding a staff that looked ancient. At this point of seeing this awkward looking man, Axel thought that he had travelled back into the past about 2000 years before his time. But he soon realized that he was wrong because the man started floating on thin air. He did not walk as it was the kosher thing to do. His robe sparkled as if glitters were sprinkled all over it; he looked heavenly. He was now floating right in front of Axel.

"Hello there, my son I've been awaiting you for a very long time, more than you could ever imagine. My name is Magi and you're standing in the realm of the otherworld where earth's ancient spirits dwell after being transformed."

Axel backed away a few steps as Magi said these words.

"Do not be afraid my son I mean you no harm."

CHAPTER 7

The place the elemental and the human were standing seemed to be a very serene place with lush vegetation. It was as if they were in a new world; water gushed out of a waterfall and the birds nestled on the trees sang sweet melodies that rhymed with the fountain that sprung out of the earth. Even the air that rushed into the lungs of Axel was fresh and he felt as though he never felt before being quite rejuvenating. Magi drew very close to Axel and extended his arms to him as a sign of welcome. Axel now felt a strange sense of warmness he had never felt before for none other than his father. He now knew that the gracious godly looking man meant him no harm but friendship. Magi took a deep gaze into the eyes of Axel and fleetingly read his mind. With this psychic aura he was able to speak to Axel without opening his mouth and these words reached Axel.

"You have been chosen mere mortal, deliverer of the spirit realm from the Shadow Law elementals". Magi smiled as these words echoed in the mind of Axel.

"Wait a minute, who said that? Did you hear errmm Magi, is it?" He stumbled back and almost fell trying to survey the area they stood on, but everywhere was plain and they were the only ones standing there.

"I know you have a lot on your mind dear boy". Once again the voice came into his mind and this time he knew it was Magi talking to him. In his thought he said to himself: "How could I be so stupid he was standing right in front of me and talking to me telepathically and yet I couldn't even know that it was him. What's wrong with me, it seems my reasoning ability has reduced drastically and my movement rather is sharper than before. I remember back in Chuck's aunty house I couldn't move that fast when I was eavesdropping on the door, and then I got caught. But here physically I feel stronger and faster. What's the cause for all these strange things?"

All these thoughts Axel was having at that instant flushed into the psychic radar of Magi and he replied back to him using his telepathic ability.

"I know you have a lot on your mind my dear son, but be patient with me I'll answer all your questions in time. After all, let's do as they say patience is a virtue. Now open your mind as I am going to enlighten you about the cosmic existence of this world and how it came into being." The environment Axel and Magi were standing on began to change as Magi began his tale... things transformed and shattered like glass as it was told by the master.

***

Long ago, before the age of man, beings called the elementals ruled the earth. It was a brand new world just as you see before you right now. Somehow, it came to be that the elementals were the creators of all early life forms on earth. Thus, the elementals sought after great power as they believed no higher order being could create them. Henceforth, a quest for supreme power began among the elementals. They devised a plan that they would create beings that were large and had no minds. In a matter of no time, the dinosaurs and other earlier life forms were created. They believed that as long these beings had no minds they could not reason like they the elementals do, and thus they were the supreme rulers of the earth. The elementals were such beings that they thrived and multiplied in numbers when the life forms they created were ignorant and idle in thinking which these earlier life-forms possessed.

But somehow something happened in the world of the elementals; one of their members broke away and was forever known as Khan the Outcast. Khan realized that his fellow elementals were feeding on the mindless souls of their creation the dinosaurs. Hence, from his own flesh, Khan gave birth to a new race known as humanoids. With the passage of time this new species evolved and divided into a subset of races. These humans were different from the dinosaurs and other earlier life-forms as they had minds that could reason and comprehend just like the elementals. To reduce the power of the elementals, Khan stole the sacred three shards of the elementals and brought the end of the dinosaurs and early life-forms that walked the earth. In natural terms on earth, this was seen as a massive asteroid that hit the earth and killed all large creations of the elementals.

Khan did this for the sole reason that the humans could thrive without the dinosaurs terrifying and killing the humans and other smaller animals. The elementals were furious with the actions of Khan and therefore sought out to destroy him. But before they could achieve their aim, Khan created a new type of elementals known as the White Lighters that fed on the enlightenment of the humans. And as a result, I was one of the few that were born. Pure and original elementals like Khan dwell on the sustenance of ignorance, lack of knowledge and innovation by the creatures that they put on the earth and that includes humans as well.

As you may know from history, earlier human forms were highly primitive and this marked the era that the Shadow Law elementals evolved and thrived, and were thus very successful in their rule of the earth. In the eyes of Master Khan, he abhorred the primitive nature of the Shadow Law elementals' creation and that is why humans are the only beings in this universe that can reason and adapt to its environment more than any other creation that the shadow law elementals ever created. To sum it all up, shadow law elementals dwell on the lack of knowledge of their creation whereas we the white lighters dwell on man's burst of knowledge, therefore we see ignorance and lack of reasoning as a sign of deprivation caused by the shadow law.

You, Axel McAllister have been chosen for this purpose of creating the vessel that would enable teleportation. We the white lighters will help you on your journey. It is not going to be an easy task since the element known as the x-factor has been repossessed by the shadow law. We must get it back from their grasp if we ever want the human race to learn how to teleport. Once you the humans learn of this new ability, it would lead to a burst of knowledge and thus bring the demise of the shadow law.

***

In the wake of the moment without any warning the barrier Magi was using to communicate with Axel broke loose with a full force as though their conversation was being monitored. Only one being in the universe was able to do that and it didn't mean good for the human race as the Shadow law elementals were making plans to seize power once again from the white lighters.

CHAPTER 8

There was a splash of water against a surface as if someone was trying to get rid of an unwanted dog. It barked as the person did this, strangely enough a girl walked towards the dog and started screaming at it.

"Oi, snap out of it." Chuck slapped his friend on the chick as these words left his mouth.

Axel woke up as if he had been startled and shrugged his shoulders.

"Where is he? And where am I?" Axel inquired worriedly as if something had gone wrong.

"Don't worry Axel you are safe in the dorm room, alright? Come on now calm down. He explained everything I needed to know." Chuck raised his friend up the bed as he said this.

"What do you mean, dude, who are you talking about? Wait a minute; don't tell me you possibly overheard everything Magi told me."

"Hey come on relax, I didn't exactly hear your conversations alright but it seems he talked to me in my head about the teleport device and that we were close to getting back the x-factor. It all makes sense, Axel."

"What do you mean it all makes sense huh? What did he exactly tell you?" Axel sounded desperate at this point.

"Well, dude instead of expecting some miracle on how to recover the x-factor from the informant who lost it to those thugs. I think it's quite clear that Magi wants you to actually create your own x-factor." Chuck blurted out confidently.

"That's very impossible, Chuck. You know very well that the x-factor is an element that hasn't been discovered yet. That is why the Shadow Law has it in their possession. Magi told me that the longer it remains with them, the more ignorant we humans become and the more powerful the Shadow elementals become." Axel looked a bit confused and unsure.

"Ah, I see... he told me you would say that. My dear friend do not be distressed, we have something at our advantage that the shadow law or whatever they call themselves in this world not have." As he said this he picked up a blank sheet and started drawing up complex algorithms and the missing link they needed in fabricating their own element.

"Wow, how did you do that? You know what Chuck you never cease to amaze me. Don't tell me he also handed you the design of the x-factor? Axel took up the sheet as Chuck finished scribbling the final touch to the design.

"This is amazing! I never for once wondered that something so complex could have a simple formula like this design as you have so put it. You are a genius man. We have to start work now. We have little time on our hands. And at this time its not just earth that needs saving but also the world that created earth itself."

***

Clouds gathered over the horizon and it seemed it was about to rain. Deep in one of the physics labs was a sophomore girl seriously concentrating on solving how to bend light rays with the body so as to prevent sun burns that were brought about as a result of tanning. The girl actually was interested not in the reasons people had for tanning. But she felt it was a problem worthy of being looked into. She was apt in her study of biophysics and this occupied her mind day after day. The lab was completely deserted and it seemed to her that this was a perfect time to engage in solar fusion solution. Also in the same room was a machine that could create objects sort of like a CAD/CAM.

All of a sudden, there was a commotion that drew the attention of the unknown girl. As soon as she realized that she wouldn't be alone very soon. She put off all the equipment and rearranged the lab back to the way it was. And foreseeing that it was extremely late, she decided to hide in one of the huge cabinets that contained toxic chemicals. Moreover, it was campus policy to prohibit personal use of the lab at awkward times and permission had to be granted for any student to use it accordingly without any restrictions.

Along the corridor walked the two bright men who seemed stoutly sure and uncompromising at the challenging task ahead of them. They took creepily steps as they didn't also want to be discovered at this dreadful night. Finally, they reached the door of LAB 312, related to the field of biophysics researches. Just as they were about to unlock the door and enter, the wind blew it right wide open.

"Wow, what's that all about, huh? I thought you said the lab is usually closed at these hours." Axel shrugged off his shoulders and walked right inside the room.

"Don't worry man I think the lab keeper just forgot to lock up after work. You know it's very tiring keeping an eye on all these labs."

"Never mind that dude, let's just get what we came looking for, alright! I have really had it with you and your lack of better judgment. For heaven's sake, we could be expelled from the university and lose our membership rights as a result of your carelessness, Chuck." At this moment, Axel directed his torchlight after rebuking his friend.

"Oh dude, not only are the doors left open but some of the cabinets have also been left open as well. Something is not right here. Ah well, never mind that let's factorize the new equation into the CAD/CAM and formulate the device." Chuck took the words of his friend seriously and started punching digits on the console of the machine. He did this really at ease as if he actually knew the coordinates for the design. The machine seemed to be in full function and with time the design they were after was slowly emerging out of the machine.

On the other side of the room, Axel was going through the cabinets one by one looking for a chemical compound called titanium oxide. He already found a bunch of other chemicals that he put in his backpack. Just as he approached the last cabinet his torchlight started fading and it became very deem.

"What the bloody hell is wrong with this thing?" He shook the torch and hit it on the surface as if that would make the light come back but it didn't.

"Oi Chuck, throw me your torch for a second, will you? The batteries in mine are dead." Axel placed the defunct torch on the floor as he caught the other torch that Chuck threw over to him. He took a tight grasp on the torch and proceeded to open the cabinet. But as he opened the final cabinet, he realized that it contained aprons and work robes instead of chemicals. Deep within the midst of the robes hid the girl. She stood really stiff and quiet as she didn't want to be found out.

Axel closed the final cabinet and walked towards Chuck who was heavily consumed in the blueprint design. He had almost finished which gave him a smirk on his face. The CAD/CAM machine was now finalizing the design which was almost complete. But just then, they both heard two pairs of foot-steps heading towards the lab that they were in. Their hearts started racing, they had to move now and quickly, because the guards were almost there.

"We got to hide right now before they get here." Chuck didn't have to be told twice. He halted the operations of the machine and put it on stand-by.

"Where are we going, dude? We can't just hide under the tables, they would surely see us." Chuck looked weary as he said this.

"Don't worry, I have an idea." They fleetingly dashed to the last cabinet, opened it and entered it right away. Luckily it was huge enough to hold the two of them. Just right at that moment the door to the lab opened and in stepped two men in black suits. They were not the usual guards on campus. They observed the room for a while and started talking to each other. Axel tried to get a good look at them but it was so dark in the room that he couldn't even make up their faces. Chuck also tried to look through the cabinet hole but it gave way for Axel only. He tried to hear what the men were talking about but it all proved futile.

"Damn it, I can't hear a word they are saying." He backed away from the cabinet door and as he did so he stepped on something. "Sorry Chuck" Axel whispered.

"Hey!" There was a sharp faint voice that came from behind the two of them. To their amazement they realized there was a third party amongst their midst. She was hidden deep within the robes. Slowly she came out looking much shaken with an air of sobriety.

"What are the two of you doing here?" She quickly whispered to them.

"What do you mean? We should be asking you the same question." Chuck whispered as if he was alarmed of some sort.

"Shut up both of you! They are still there alright. We have to be very quiet because they seem to be looking around now." Axel peeped through the cabinet slit as the two suspicious men started examining the room as if in caution. In the huge cabinet they kept very quiet as one of the agents was close to them. He drew his hand to open it, as he did so his partner yelled at him.

"There is nothing here, agent 18. We must leave here immediately before we draw attention to our operation." The man close to the cabinet that contained Axel, Chuck and the girl backed away and murmured something to himself. Axel was close by and could infer that the man was very displeased that they had to leave.

Both men exited the lab and Axel saw that there was a flash of light in the corridor; in a matter of seconds they were gone.

CHAPTER 9

The CAD/CAM machine was still on stand-by and the design had to be completed. Chuck paced forward to it and started punching the console. He initialized the finalising of the blueprint design. Axel took his backpack and inspected its contents to see if he had everything in order. The girl now looked calm but was still unsure of who the young lads were.

"Hello there, my name is Amber, what's yours?" Her voice sounded croaky as if she had been talking for hours. Axel raised his hand to shake her.

"Thanks a lot for not giving us away, I'm Axel and that's Chuck." Chuck nodded as Axel called his name in unison.

"Well, it's not as if we were not in this together. If we three were both caught, we would all be expelled for what we... ammm excuse me I meant what were you two up to in this lab." Amber also had a backpack and she propped it up behind her.

"Hey, look here will you? What we are doing here is none of your business; just as we don't bother to ask you as well." Just as Axel said this he noticed one of Amber's factor equations on the molecules of the body which were involved in the manipulation of light. He was very impressed by this coincidence since they were also after the same thing. Thinking to himself, he decided to ask what her objective was about the equations but he stopped as he realized that he was rude to her. So adopting a bit of a more pragmatic approach, he decided to apologize to her and then inquire about the equation.

"Hey Amber, look I'm sorry for being rude to you just now, you know it's because we are working on a covert operation that could end one day saving humanity. Strange things have happened to us lately and it would drive you even insane just by imagining them. I guess history keeps toying with us since it brings back the old and makes it new again. Look the point is I think we are after the same thing here. And we need to work together." He looked astounding compromised and yet unflinching as these words left his mouth.

"Oh 'we', what do you mean by that, huh? Just a moment ago, you said I had no business in knowing what you are up to, and now you talk about 'we'. You have to do a lot better than that if you want me to join the gang." Amber paced back and forth in a circular fashion around Axel as she made her point quite clear.

"Hey, point of correction Missy... this is no gang as you put it. This is an experiment that people would kill just to get their hands on. We are talking about something beyond this world far above your imagination, so you can't stand here and brag about your factorial equation..." Chuck sounded a bit mad at Amber but he took the design he had made with ease and put in his backpack.

"Hush Chuck, you haven't seen her equation and you are already at her throat." Axel whispered Amber's equation into Chuck's ears and his eyes shone with amazement.

"No way, you don't mean it. How could she have done that? You don't think that Magi might have sent her, do you reckon... oh well, I guess now we have to invite her on board the mission impossible now turned possible." Chuck giggled a bit but kept his cool.

"What are two talking about and what is this mission you blabbing about?" Amber retorted.

"Well, you'll see it yourself when we show it to you at the Musket Club at 7pm. If you decide to join me that is errr... I mean us." The manner in which Axel said this seemed that he was sincere in inviting her to join them.

"Wow, ok I accept, it's a date. At 7 it is. She swung her backpack behind herself and left. Chuck marvelled at the incredible air in which she did this.

"It's time we leave this place, Chuck. We have a lot of work on our hands and let's just keep our heads up because we have double date."

"Hey you mean triple date. After all it's the three of us... man what I would give to know how she came out with those equations. I mean we could use it in aiding the fusion that body needs to be destroyed and created again." Chuck and Axel walked along the other labs in the corridor and finally exited the building to get ready for the experiment and not to mention the new friend or foe they had met who could either aid or annihilate the cause of saving humanity.

***

The Musket Club was one of the most popular pubs on campus as it was the centre of fraternities and sororities' social engagements. They usually had elegant ways of displaying their good food and drinks which were quite attractive to the general population of the entire student body. Their meals were just great. And usually young blokes would bring their dates to the abode of the Musket. The Musket as it was so called because of an old legend that had it that deep within the grounds of the university was buried the golden musket. If relinquished and fired instead of taking a life and it rather reverses the person's health back to normal and henceforth sealing the person's death in its shells. However, these days no one or student even believes in the legend since the university grounds have been thoroughly excavated but no golden musket has ever been found. But the original owners of the club still believes that it exists thus their naming it so to keep the faith alive and inspire young hopefuls who seek its awesome power in reversing death.

The mood in the Musket Club that evening was that of a calm and cosy one. Almost everyone was engaging another in a conversation whiles drinking beer. Along one of the tables patiently sat Amber, she looked very cute in her blue dress with a little bit of make-up. She sipped her beer and checked her time, twisting her head from side to side since it got into her face. Just then right at that moment in walked Axel, he rushed to the table that Amber looking terribly guilty since he had delayed.

"Hmmm, it seems you are late, aren't you? And where's your friend? I thought both of you were coming together." She picked up the menu as she said that looking quite pleased with herself.

"What can I say? I really am sorry about the lateness. I had a bit of a rough time putting certain things together for this rendezvous. And Chuck is still tied up in it. We have a lot of work on our hands you see. Few can counter the skill with which you wrote those equations, I must say I was very impressed when I saw it." Just then he paused as he told the waiter that he wanted the same beer that Amber was having.

"Well, to tell you the truth I don't really know. I wouldn't want to you to think I was relying on intuition like most women do because that's not the reason for it. I would say it's something more complex and of a delicate matter, one that would drive an average man insane. The bare thought of it is more or less enough to do this, I believe." Amber looked quite serious and tossed her head from side to side still maintaining eye-contact with Axel.

"I see then, I believe Chuck and I are not alone in this cause. Let's join forces and see our ambitions come true whatever both our aims are." Axel extended his hands to hers and she received it warmly without any hesitation.

CHAPTER 10

The mood was set as the three young hopeful started their plans of creating the vessel of teleportation. They had all the ingredients to see the machine work without fault. The machine Chuck was working on with the CAD/CAM design template was now complete. They mixed the chemicals that they had nicked from the lab, and everything was starting to look as it was meant to be. They used their dorm room as the grounds for the experiment. They also did their homework on past researches like their own and knew how dangerous it was going to get. The point was that for any living thing to teleport, it meant it had be destroyed and recreated again. They knew that they couldn't use themselves before they were absolutely sure a human being could partake in it, they pondered on the thought of not violating any ethical issues that could pose a threat to the experiment. For that the three thought of using mice that terrorized the dorm room, and they weren't hard to find and catch at all. The x-factor was now ready for use and the new element they had manufactured. The three decided to start the experiment right after their classes was over, in order not to raise suspicion on their intentions. They parted to their own ways and all promised to make it back at the dorm before midnight.

***

Far on the other realm of the shadows, there was a huge stir in their moods as they swirled in their smoke that turned black. Whenever, they turned the colour black it meant that humans were on the brink of discovering something that would forever improve their lives. Henceforward, as this incident took place they became vulnerable and decrepit. Once again they gathered on the mountain top of their world. But they were not alone, far opposite the mountain was another smoke which looked very pale and white as snow. The huge white smoke split into seven different parts and right at the top was Magi who led the six other white lighters. As the white lighters gazed onto the shadows, these words left Magi:

"It's time you became extinct, primitive souls of the damned, attack now!" Right after Magi said this; the other six white lighters moved violently and attacked the shadows that were in the hundreds. It seemed that the white lighters were outnumbered but that did not stop them. Smoke after smoke merged with thick black smoke as it did so it burned right out into oblivion.

The fight was now on and it just got started. At this moment it seemed that Magi and his white lighters were winning as the shadows kept blowing up into oblivion.

***

Back on earth, in the dorm of Axel and Chuck with the aid of Amber, the experiment to teleport had just begun. The apparatus was set as the lab mouse was also caught ready to partake in the experiment. The mouse was caged and looked as if it was frightened of some sort, it squeaked at every turn and movement that the three experimenters made. The teleport device had now been completed and it needed to be tested. Amber added the finishing touches to it by factorizing her equation to the design. Now with the aid of the x-factor, they wondered whether it could absolutely work without any setbacks. They were going to find out. Axel had the feeling that now they were on the brink of a huge scientific breakthrough, the world of the elementals was at war; he could feel it in his very veins that Magi and the white lighters were indeed outnumbered by the shadows.

He now felt that he was the sole determinant in the war; the teleport device had to work before the white lighters could win the war.

Chuck was now punching the console of the teleport and set the distance the mouse would travel to 6 feet. Axel removed the mouse out of its cage and placed it in the centre of the device. Amber looked quite nervous and wondered whether it would really work as planned. As she stood there in a nervous wreck, Axel took hold her hands and whispered these words to her.

"Don't worry, everything will be fine." Just as these words left his mouth, Chuck pressed the button, and the mouse started to glow. In an instant, it vanished nowhere to be seen. The three young hopefuls were amazed at the outstanding result. But they had to find where the mouse had disappeared to, suddenly two men dressed in black suit appeared out of nowhere, and one of them was holding the mouse.

"Is this what you are looking for? Well we have it right here... come and have it." Just as he spoke these words, agent 17 squeezed the life out of the poor mouse. In a matter of seconds the mouse stopped moving as the life left its body. Agent 17 then dropped it on the floor, agent 18 however moved closer to where Axel and Amber stood, he slid his hand into his jacket and brought something that looked like a gun. Axel stared at it without flinching and realized that it was the same men that were responsible for his father's death. Now, he realized that it was he they were after. His blood boiled at the thought of attacking the men or whatever they were, but he had to think twice as they were holding guns now. He needed to act fast as these guys didn't look like they were about to play around. Chuck froze the moment the 18 pointed the gun at him.

"Stop what you're doing all of you! One move and we won't hesitate in shooting you. You humans are funny creatures aren't you? The moment you invent something new we the shadow elementals become weak. This is all due to the fallen shadow Master Khan and his son, Magi. But he is no more, and we thrived in his absence. Until you inevitably showed up with your foolish ideas of teleporting, we had to seize the moment of killing you since you pose a serious threat to our very existence." Agent 17 now paused and stared at Axel.

"Do you remember me, my dear Axel McAllister?" A wicked grin moved down 17's face as he shrugged off his shoulders and removed his dark sunglasses.

"Yes, I do know who both of you are. I remember that day as a young boy my father took me fishing, and both of you appeared and murdered him. There was not a single piece of him left anywhere. Back then, I did not fully understand how it was possible that the two of were able to do this. Now I do know that both of you are not of this world, and the bodies you inhabit does neither age nor exist." The anger in Axel started to show in his voice and he soon clenched his fist ready to do some serious damage.

"Hmmm, don't get ahead of yourself, boy. You think you can take me with both your bare hands. Come on then, let's see what you are made of." Agent 17 took out his gun and placed it on the table. 18 was however amazed that the boy would take on his superior, this gave him a huge smirk on his face. But he did not lose focus on guarding Chuck and Amber who were very cautious at this point.

The fight was now on and it was 17 who threw the first punch. Axel did well enough to dodge it and he counterattacked with a kick that could make an average man howl in pain but 17 stood there smiling at him.

"I'm quite surprised that a runt like yourself can do what you just did right now but let me give you a little secret, my dear boy. Shadows who inhabit humans do not feel pain, needless to say that the more you hit me the stronger I become. You humans are pathetic, now take this!" With that he sent Axel a punch that sent him half across the room.

Axel seemed to be in serious pain as he landed next to a table, whereas 17 laughed in an evil manner as if he was invincible. But there was a catch; somewhere lying on the table next to him was the gun.

"Now 18, kill them all!" 17 screamed at the top of his voice.

"Not so fast, put the gun down." Axel made it to his feet and pointed his weapon at 18, ready to shoot. At that very moment, 17 moved so fast that it made everyone to start shooting at each other. There were flashes of light everywhere. Chuck took cover behind a book-shelf and placed one of the teleport devices on his hands. Amber was close-by Axel as he fired repeatedly to keep them at bay. He then called out to Chuck:

"Chuck, factor a location off campus and get us out of here, now!" Chuck did as he was told although in a very hasty manner. He timed the machine to teleport in 10 seconds and he dashed half-way across the room to Axel and Amber. 18 shot in the direction that Chuck went in. And in a matter of seconds, the three disappeared completely into the unknown.

CHAPTER 11

There was a rumbling of stones in what seemed to be a cove. The waves washed ashore as the three looked awestruck. One question resounding in their heads was where in the world were they? And were they safe from those two thugs? But somehow Axel knew the answer to these questions unbeknownst to the two. They paced about trying to check the environment they had appeared in.

"Well, one thing is for certain... we are very far from campus grounds." Chuck blurted out but he didn't seem convinced enough. Amber looked alarmed as well as she realized that her thoughts about the machine came to pass. How this was possible she could not fathom it. There was a solemn expression on her face as she knew that Axel was sure of the place they were. And this soon came to pass as Axel confirmed her thoughts.

"I do know where we are and you are not going to like it. It's apparent that Chuck took us very far from school but that was not the only thing that happened. I think Magi intervened and brought us into his world."

"No way, that's impossible Axel... I thought you said he only existed in your dreams and thoughts. Besides the device only works on earth and it's bound by its laws." Chuck said this to reason with his friend.

"Wait a minute both of you. Please tell me what's going on. So far you two keep talking about stuff that I can't relate with..." Just before she said another word Chuck cut her off.

"This has nothing to do with you so butt out of it." But before he too could finish talking a man in white robes appeared to them. And Axel blurted out aloud: "Magi"

"But you are wrong young one, this matter has everything to do with the young lady. For if it was not have been her help you would not have obtained the key to teleportation. You must learn to choose your words wisely young lad for the path of the chosen trio shall not be an easy one to tread." Magi moved sharply between them as these words left him although his lips didn't move as sounded in their minds by means of telepathy.

"Wow, this isn't happening... you are floating and I can hear you in my mind without you talking. I didn't know telepathy was also possible." Amber pinched herself to check if she wasn't dreaming.

"Well, my dear everything is possible only if you believe in it earnestly and yes, this is happening and I'm glad to tell you that all your dreams, aspirations and expectations are all one thing and interconnected. Everything that you think about can become reality. And the quest of it becoming reality rest on the actions you take, I believe it's time to unravel the mysteries that has plagued you all since you pondered upon this adventure. I know it's not been an easy one but I'll let you know that it was indeed worth it.

I am an elemental being who has taken on human form like those agents who tried to disrupt your plans and also kill you. Before this moment, there was a war we the white lighters waged on the shadow elementals who are known as the shadow law organization back on earth. But unlike us, they can take on human form and wreck havoc on your planet. But we the white lighters can only exist in our own world and in the figment of your imaginations in which we dwell.

Anyways, the war is not over yet... although we lost today's battle we are still a force to reckon with.

It was, fearing that last action that is why I brought you into my world. It is a world between the elemental realm and that of earth. Strangely enough in human terms it does not exist but thanks to the liberator of white light elementals by the first elder known as Master Khan who forged this realm out of his elemental form. And thus, we were born the neo-white light elementals as a result."

Right at the moment, the ground the three stood on began to tumble as a strong whirlpool surrounded all of them and the current of the sea rose to a very high level. And out of this whirlpool came out sparks of light that immediately metamorphosed into people in the likeness of the Magi. Their numbers were few and they grouped around Magi looking at the three visitors smiling.

At this point, Axel realised that these were the neo-white lighters that Magi just spoke about and all that they saw and felt were all parts of their creator, who was referred as Master Khan. The same feeling happened to Amber as well although she wasn't all that sure what the right questions to ask were, nevertheless she was somehow at ease that these things were real, and that she wasn't just imagining any of it. On the other hand, Chuck felt quite lost and a little indifferent, and yet he felt overjoyed like the rest. Sensing their eager questions Magi started to talk in the heads again.

"Yes, my friends those agents called 17 and 18 are shadow law elementals in human forms on earth where we do not exist but only they can. They have existed far before us and their being is woven into the making the earth and other planets with no life force. They invade a planet and feed on its inhabitants draining them by depriving them of knowledge and feeding them with ignorance. And for a while now they have planet earth in their sights. They want nothing more than seeing that the earth is destroyed and no remnant is left behind. They want to kill you three because you hold the key to their doom. And this is the power of teleportation. For with this power they fear you may be able to break into their realm and put an end to their tyranny.

In this world of Khan, they cannot hear or see you. That is why I've brought you here so that I may enlighten you further and also to keep you safe. You three have been able to learn how to teleport and this would not go well in the shadow realm. They would stop at nothing to put an end to your plans and see to it that it does not materialize but you must not give up. This is because you have us the white lighters to guard you on your journey of bringing teleportation to the human race. I bid you all farewell for the teleport conspiracy has begun. Go now and fight for us all, for remember that we are behind you.

CHAPTER 12

Within a split second the three had disappeared and were back on earth. They appeared right in front of the main administration of the university campus of Warwick. It was marked by busy students heading for their classes and others hurrying to meet appointments at a library. The mood on campus seemed indifferent as if it had not noticed that three people had appeared.

As the trio suddenly realized the realities of their mission, it became apparent to them the gravity of the task they had to perform. For, Axel it meant that the tremendous work that he and Chuck put together in bringing their dreams had been achieved. Not forgetting the assistance of Amber's brilliant contribution. But somehow the young inventor now knew that there were forces in search of what they had so badly that they would stop at nothing to get their hands on it, even to the point of killing innocent people. However, he could also see that they were not alone and from the very start the white elementals were assisting them all along. He could now fathom it that it was them who put the idea in his mind in the first place. All this time there was a secret plot to stop man from teleporting and using abilities that only gods were believed to possess. It was now up to the three young hopefuls to deliver mankind from this hardship of normal transport system made up of aircraft, vehicles and ships that have robbed people of their lives. Many have periled in this out-dated system of transport and now the trio would usher in the dawn of teleportation.

"We have created a vessel that may be flawless yet, however a hazardous task is upon us now. I know that all three of us are students and that our daily studying obligations outweigh all our other priorities, but I want you to know this if we succeed in revealing this invention to the world we wouldn't have to worry about school anymore. Rather we would build a new system of acquiring knowledge that would thrive on the world of Khan. You saw those elementals and what they were all about."

At that moment, they all started laughing and all seemed well. But lurking in a narrow passage not too far from them were agents 18 and 17. They seemed to be distraught and furious; their weapons had been taken from them and could not fatally wound the enemies without them. Hence, they devised a plan to secretly steal back their weapons and then kill them.

Night had befallen the campus grounds, and almost everyone had retreated to their dorm rooms and were either asleep or studying maybe for a following day quiz. The same was for Axel and Chuck, as it was obvious they had missed a few lectures they needed some catching up and explanations to give their hall master and lecturers. As they pondered about their plans about what they should be doing tomorrow to reveal their plans to the world, Chuck stumbled across something unfamiliar in his backpack and realized what they were. Somehow he realized it was the guns that agents had tried shooting them with. Chuck then wondered how on earth that there were two guns in the backpack without them was taking it. Although he however, knew back in the scuffle with the shadow hosts, Axel had one of the guns.

Just at that moment, Axel entered the room looking a bit confused about the course of action to take tomorrow and how they were going to break the news to the general public. Right then Chuck thought about asking Axel about the extra gun, but seeing the worry on his friend's face, he decided to drop the subject. However, surprising enough Axel rather brought the subject on.

"I see you might be guessing at what they are" Axel told his friend.

"I do know what they are but they seem to be cool looking. I do think they can be fired and those villains got really scared when they realised you had their gun." Chuck tried using it and examining it in every possible way but he just couldn't get enough of its sly looking appearance. He then proceeded and fired it at a can coke that lay on the table. Within an instant the can was vaporised.

"Wow, cool!" Chuck blurted out.

Remember these agents are shadow hosts will be in need of their guns, and thus the longer we have them the safer we are, I reckon."

"It's so cool how you fired it when we were back in there with all those flashes of light, and strangely enough you also got hold of the other agent's gun, awesome mate!" Chuck said this amazed.

"Well, you know to be honest Magi aided me a little bit, but still thanks for the interest Chuck. You see I realized this as he teleported us into his realm. I think Magi can possess objects that the shadow elementals can use." Axel paced back and forth thinking and finally said this:

"We have to focus on delivering this invention to the board as I've already spoken with our research supervisor. He said he would lend his support throughout our demonstration of the machine we created. Can you believe that?" Axel confided in Chuck but he looked a bit weary.

"Well it's quite obvious he wants a bit of the glory when we demonstrate tomorrow, although we might need Amber to factor in the equations again for it to work again." Chuck dashed straight to the bed as these words left him.

"What...? I thought we designed the machine to save equations through the cubits we installed." Axel glanced at the machine.

"Oh well, it doesn't seem to work like that, mate. All atomic systems keep on changing from one time to another, so they are never stable. The cubit factored by Amber was the one we needed at that particular time for the mouse to teleport. But one thing I've got to ask. How were you able to acquire the two guns from those agents?" Chuck enquired from his friend.

"I don't really know for sure but one thing I do know for sure is that I only took one gun from the table I fell beside to. I don't know how two of them got in the backpack.

After a while, when Axel and Chuck fell asleep, the door leading to their room slowly opened and in walked two dark figures. Although, it was pitch dark in the room, they still wore shady black glasses. How they could see in the dark was still a mystery in itself. Agent 17 glanced at the room Axel was in whiles 18 foolishly .snooped around in search of the guns.

"Watch it, no noise! Otherwise, they would know we are here. I wouldn't let them have the satisfaction that we powerless without our guns. First, we get the guns and then we kill them." 17 whispered to 18.

Just then agent 17 saw the teleport devise and he took it.

It did not take long for them to find the guns and with a gloated look on their faces. 17 and 18 sensed the guns as if the guns were an extension to their bodies. They now approached the backpack that contained their guns. At this moment, as they attempted taking their weapons, something extraordinary happened: A ring of light burst open and knocked out the two agents at the same. The hit was so powerful that it sent them flying through the walls of the dorms and right outside onto the pavement. Had it been a human who had been knocked out by such a force, it would have meant instant death before even hitting the pavement floor on the streets. But these two agents apparently were not human but something much more formidable. They simply got up although, however, one of them appeared to have been injured by the fall. For it was a two storey fall. They touched each other and in moments, they were gone.

At that moment, the bang on the wall woke almost every student on that block of that dorm. Axel woke up Chuck, as it seemed he was in a deep sleep. Chuck got up and walked to the opposite end of his bed.

"Oi, Axel! There is a hole in my wall. Come look quick!" Chuck screamed but his friend was already there.

"That's not the only thing that's happened mate. The teleport devise is gone."

CHAPTER 13

The Scotland Yard were in the dorm where the crime scene had taken place in a matter of moments, and they took the two boys in for questioning. And they were released without much provocation as the police found that their account was beyond reasoning with. The weather outside the police station appeared to turn grey as this was a sign that rain was coming. The two blokes were not the least concerned about the police detectives that interrogated them, but the rather their presentation of their machine was gone and with no clue where it had been taken. Although they knew that the agents had taken it. The only thing they weren't sure of was where they had taken it and would they destroy it since it was in their best interest if mankind never knew how to teleport. They were very troubled indeed not to say that the research board would be sitting in just a few hours to see their presentation. But where was Amber? As they also needed her help to for the machine to work accordingly.

Chuck earlier on phoned Amber and as she couldn't pick, the young lads decided to pay her a visit. They took to their heels as the board would be sitting very soon. They had little time to lose so they rushed along campus streets dorm after dorm, trying to locate hers. Although, they hadn't visited her before, somehow it felt as they already had been there as they soon found the place. Immediately, as they knocked on the door, a girl opened it and she looked as distraught as any living person they had ever seen.

"Hello there, we're looking for Amber?" Axel inquired from the girl who appeared to be Amber's roommate.

"Oh my word, please come in quick!" She hurriedly tucked them inside and started talking very fast.

"You won't believe this... but emmm... Amber has been kidnaped by two guys in a suit. They said they would kill her if I told the police about it. And that I should be expecting you two to give this message." She held out a piece of paper and gave it to them.

Axel and Chuck both looked at each other and said aloud: "THE AGENTS!"

Axel opened the paper and on it was scribbled these:

We've the teleport devise and your girl. Bring our weapons to us or we kill her. Don't try any tricks... we know you need her for the devise to work. We'll be waiting at the football pitch at your school. Do well, not to alert the Scotland Yard for they can't stop us... Be warned.

"We have to save her and fast." Axel blurted out. "Listen here, these men are not what they seem and can be very dangerous so we got to do as they say" The girl looked scared as Axel told her this. "Although, there is one thing you can do for us. Did Amber tell you what we about to do? I mean the demonstration of our experiment."

"Yes, she did... she was just getting prepared when those thugs grabbed her. Please do try to save her, I've got a feeling you can save." The roommate replied.

"Hmmm, there is one thing... though. We need your help. We need you to stall the research board when it gets to our turn. We would try to make it before then. Can you do that for us?" Axel crumbled the note as he said this.

"Sure thing, don't worry I've got you covered. Just go and save her." With those words, the young lads left the dorm and headed for their own to get the weapons. They started running and right past the auditorium where the demo was to take place.

"Mate, don't you think this could be a trap? We've to think twice before handing out those guns to the agents." Chuck sounded worried but Axel assured him otherwise.

"I know mate but I've a plan and plus I think we've got Magi on our side. Remember, what he said?"

About that moment, they had got to the steps outside the dorm. The area was packed with students who had heard about the incident of the hole in the wall the night before. As Chuck and Axel passed by they overheard one of the students saying that the hole might have been caused by UFOs since the roommates of the dorms were working on a secret project. Right then, as one of them made out Axel, they came closer in their groups wanting a piece of the action.

"Oi laddies, aren't you both supposed be demonstrating to the research boards? I heard your invention is slated for today and you are still here." He asked Axel. He appeared to look tall and extremely muscle-bound with a beard that was well trimmed. Right that instant, an idea struck up in Axel's head and he smiled.

"I've got a plan but we would need his help." Axel told Chuck as the lad came forward licking his lips.

"Yes, you're right, mate but I think we would need your help." Axel told the fellow and there was a huge grin on his face.

"Well, I would be damned... didn't think a pair of intellectuals like yourselves would be needing my help. Anyways I accept. The name's Mordred and at your service." Chuck then paced to the room to get the guns and Axel then asked Mordred another request.

"Nice to meet you, Mordred... I would be much obliged if your friends could join us too."

Moments later Chuck came along with the guns in his backpack. And they all headed for the football pitch.

CHAPTER 14

As they made their way to the known forces ahead of them, Axel couldn't help but realize how the gun was able to fire back in the lab room but would not fire now that they really needed. He pondered on the thought that whether Magi could help them get out of this trouble. These agents were extremely annoyed and would want nothing less than see them all dead. By now the three young lads were getting nearer to the rendezvous, to Chuck it seemed to him that they were walking into a trap that they had no way of escaping. There was not a single soul in sight as they arrived at the stadium, the pitch on which the rugby players practised on looked as if it had already kept and maintained properly as was everything else. Before they entered Axel laid the plan to his friends, but would it work? Axel knew that the agents thought it was just them two were coming to Amber's rescue, he decided to use the element of surprise to do away with agents for good and retrieve the teleport devise they had worked so hard for years. Underneath all the boldness of his actions, he also felt a longing to be with Amber and see to it that nothing happened with her. He knew that he had not felt like this with any girl he had ever met. It was their fault Amber got into this mess, and he didn't know what he would do to himself if he could not save her.

"Mordred, there is one thing you should know before we enter the stadium. These guys are not what they seem to be, they may look human but they are not. I want you to take this backpack and head for the control room above the stadium." Axel told him and patted Chuck's back.

"Are you sure, mate? I thought you needed me to make mince meat out of these blokes or whatever they are." Mordred said this looking puzzled as if he wanted some action, he really thought he could use the agents as punching bags but all he same he did as he was told.

With Mordred headed for the control room, Axel and Chuck finally made it inside the stadium and just as they thought the two agents were in the middle of the pitch with the same smug look on their faces. Amber was sitting on the ground with her hands and feet tied with a rope. She looked quite happy to see her friends, and Axel was happy she was alright.

"Wait... wait a minute, don't take another step. Where are the guns? You are indeed very foolish boys not to bring the guns. I thought I made myself clear that bring the guns along with you. Well, now you watch as I kill your girl and then I would finish the two of you." Agent 17 looked quite very annoyed but still kept his composure as he drew a dagger out of his suit.

"Hold on there, I don't think you are going to kill anyone of us just yet. I can see that's why you need your guns. You are powerless without them, that's why both of you were knocked out of our rooms last night. Yes you were able to take the teleport devise but were not able to take your guns because Magi prevented you two from taking it. How wise Magi is, isn't he?" Axel took a step closer to them as he said this looking very courageous knowing that the two agents were harmless without their weapons.

"You foolish earthlings, you never seize to amaze me..." 17 laughed cockishly and he cracked his knuckles looking at 18 who made a similar gesture. "So what... huh? You think both of you can take us two. Even without our guns, our strength far exceeds yours. So I wouldn't call it an even match since both sides stand an equal chance and in this you would both lose and the price are your worthless lives."

Chuck clenched his fists and run as fast he could towards 18. Within that instant, 17 threw his dagger in a precise aim that landed squarely in the chest of Chuck.

Axel and Amber screamed but it was too late, Chuck was bleeding on the ground in agony. Just as things were getting out of hand, everything froze as Magi appeared in the mind of Axel. Magi spoke like he never did before but knew he had brought help.

"Listen up, my son..." For that moment Axel realized that it was indeed his father who was talking with him. The father he had lost many years ago was using telepathy to communicate with him. "I know you are in shock Axel, but this is not the time and place to be, your friend is dying and the only thing that can save him is the golden musket. The musket is no ordinary gun, instead of taking a life it rather gives life."

"But father, the gun is only a myth... and nobody's ever found it and I don't have the time to go looking for it now."

"Don't worry about that son, the moment everyone unfreezes drop to the ground and touch the grass with both your hands. The golden musket will then appear and you must be quick about it. Remember this though, the golden musket has an opposite on the shadow law agents and thus killing them. Your friend must be shot point blank, and the shell would heal his wounds." With these final words, everything in the environment started be in motion again. Without much a do, Axel dropped to ground on his knees as he was told. The moment he did that, shock waves left his body and penetrated the ground. The shock was so violent that it made the ground shake. There was a sharp slit in the earth, and through the hole the golden musket appeared in broad daylight. In that instant, Axel pointed the gun at his friend in pain and fired it immediately.

This gun was extraordinary, instead of releasing a shell it rather acted like a vacuum machine. With sparks of blue light from the gun, the dagger-wound on Chuck healed as if it wasn't there in the first place.

"What... what is that?" 18 turned around and asked his fellow shadow agent. But 17 was too busy gazing at the efficacy of weapon being able to harm.

Just then right after that, Axel pointed the golden musket at 18 and fired it without a warning.

Agent 17 called out very loudly at his fellow shadow but it was too short too late, "No 18, watch out, he's pointing the gun at you.", the gun had been fired and it hit him squarely in the back. 18 started to shake and he cried out violently shaking until he finally exploded.

Just then, there was a noise close to stadium which came from the control room, agent 17 realized there was a third party to all the commotion and within moments, he teleported to the control room where Mordred was hiding. Axel fired at 17 but he was too fast for him. He realized 17 was using the teleport devise they had invented. Axel realized 17 knew the location of Mordred, without a single word he headed fro the control room above the stadium. Chuck stayed with Amber and used the dagger that stabbed him to cut to her ropes free.

By the time, Axel got to the control room Mordred laid on the ground bleeding and he looked half dead but without much effort. As Axel tried using the gun to save him, agent 17 appeared out of nowhere and knocked the gun out of Axel's hands. He then grabbed Axel's throat and raised him up. 17 then pointed his gun at Axel ready to fire.

"It is time to die, worthless earthling... now join your father." There was a sharp flash light and right that instant, Axel shouted in pain as though he had really died. The grip on Axel's throat loosened as agent 17 started crying in pain very violent and within moments he too blew into a thousand pieces never to be seen again.

As Axel balanced himself on his feet, he realized that Mordred wasn't through yet and he was holding the golden musket as if it weighed more than a ton.

Axel then took the gun from him, "Hold it mate, don't shoot me... are you mental? I just saved your life." But that didn't stop Axel and he fired it and within seconds, Mordred got better.

The teleport devise was on the floor and it looked undisturbed and ready for the presentation that was awaiting them back on campus. For that moment, it seemed all was well. The machine worked amazing well with no fault and the x-factor did its work as it should. The informant who was unable to deliver the x-factor to Axel and Chuck was also present for it was his research skills into renewable elements like the x-factor that inspire Axel to design the teleport devise. On the whole, several questions were posed to the three young inventors and they answered them with much ease.

But somehow, unknown to the rest of the world were forces involved in finally giving mankind the ability to teleport. Knowledge is power and as the three being Axel, Chuck and Amber decided to keep the world of Magi a secret, they realized that it was Magi's magic and physics that enabled all this to happen. The years would not be an easy one and the transportation revolution had just begun.

TWELVE YEARS LATER...

In this new era in mankind's history, accidents had reduced by a considerable level and were almost unknown to be a cause of death. In the streets, roads weren't needed anymore and these were replaced by gate bridges that transported people and material goods from place to place and yes in time as well. There was a close monitoring system to check crime and other matters.

The best part was this transport revolution made Axel, Chuck and Amber the richest people in the world and consequently Axel and Amber got married. They have three kids and chuck visits them from time to time.

In the distant planet of the shadow law elementals, it was no more and thus Magi's world replaced it and all was well for the teleport conspiracy was averted.

The End...